Rough Tough Rowdy

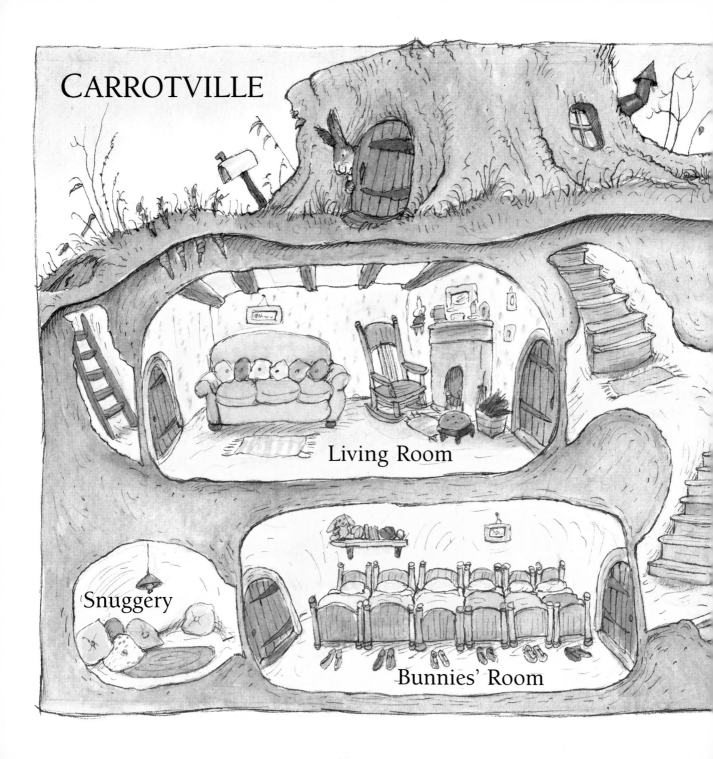

CARROTVILLE

Living Room

Snuggery

Bunnies' Room

Attic

Dining Room

Kitchen

Mama's Room

Rhoda   Ricky   Mama   Margaret   Rowdy   Rooter   Rena
                      Rabbit   Rose

ROUGH TOUGH
ROWDY

A BANK STREET BOOK ABOUT VALUES

By William H. Hooks

Illustrated by Lynn Munsinger

VIKING

VIKING
Published by the Penguin Group
Viking Penguin, a division of Penguin Books USA Inc.,
375 Hudson Street, New York, New York 10014, U.S.A.
Penguin Books Ltd, 27 Wrights Lane, London W8 5TZ, England
Penguin Books Australia Ltd, Ringwood, Victoria, Australia
Penguin Books Canada Ltd, 2801 John Street, Markham, Ontario, Canada L3R 1B4
Penguin Books (N.Z.) Ltd, 182-190 Wairau Road, Auckland 10, New Zealand

Penguin Books Ltd, Registered Offices: Harmondsworth, Middlesex, England

First published in 1992 by Viking Penguin, a division of Penguin Books USA Inc.

1 3 5 7 9 10 8 6 4 2

Series graphic design by Alex Jay/Studio J
Editor: Gillian Bucky
Special thanks to James A. Levine, and Regina Hayes

Copyright © Byron Preiss Visual Publications, Inc., 1992.

Text copyright © The Bank Street College of Education, 1992.

Illustrations copyright © Byron Preiss Visual Publications, Inc., and Lynn Munsinger, 1992.

All rights reserved

A Byron Preiss Book

Carrotville is a trademark of The Bank Street College of Education.

Library of Congress Cataloging-in-Publication Data
Hooks, William H. Rough, tough, Rowdy / by William H. Hooks ;
illustrated by Lynn Munsinger.   p.   cm.—(Carrotville ; no. 4)
"A Byron Preiss book"—CIP t.p. verso.
Summary: Rowdy the rabbit likes to punch, push, and play
rough, to the annoyance of his brothers and sisters, but
it is not until he finds himself in the company of two even
tougher rabbits that he can see what is fun and what is not.
ISBN 0-670-82868-8
[1. Rabbits—Fiction.   2. Behavior—Fiction.]   I. Munsinger,
Lynn, ill.   II. Title.   III. Series: Carrotville adventure ; no. 4.
PZ7.H7664Ro   1992   [E]—dc20   91-29257   CIP   AC

Printed in Singapore

For William Robert Davies – W.H.H.
For Carol – L.M.

Rowdy raced out of the house shouting, "Gangway, everybody! Here comes Rough Tough Rowdy!"

He bumped into Rena.

He knocked over Rooter.

And he turned Margaret Rose upside down!

"Quit it!" yelled Margaret Rose.
"You flattened my beautiful ears!"
  "Stop it! Stop it!" shouted Ricky
and Rhoda.

But Rowdy just laughed. "Aw, I was only playing," he said. "Come on, let's have a game of tag. I promise I'll be good."

He bounced over and roughly tagged Rhoda. "You're it! You're it!" Rowdy shouted.

The bunnies hopped and jumped out of Rhoda's way. Rowdy hopped higher and jumped farther than the others. He didn't look where he was going, so he kept bumping into the other bunnies. But he didn't get tagged.

Rhoda finally
caught Rooter.

Then Rooter caught
Margaret Rose.

Rough Tough Rowdy chanted:
Margaret Rose can't catch me.
I can hop as high as a tree!

He hopped so high he lost his balance and over he went.

Tap, Tap! Margaret Rose tagged Rowdy. Then she hopped away calling:

Rowdy's it,
and has a fit,
and doesn't know how
to get out of it!

Rowdy acted as if he did have a fit. He hopped so hard and he yelled so loud, and he tagged Margaret Rose so hard that he knocked her down.

"Ow!" yelled Margaret Rose. "You banged my nose. You're too rough again!"

"You can't play with us," said Rhoda. "You're too rough."

"Go away, Rowdy," shouted Rena and Ricky. "We don't want to play with you!"

Slowly Rowdy hopped away. He scowled and growled, "Aw, I was only playing. They can't take a joke. They're just scaredy baby bunnies."

"Hi, Rowdy, want to play tag with us?" someone called.

Rowdy saw Bear Cub waddling through the grass. Behind her, Young Wild Cat was pouncing on grasshoppers. Young Wild Cat and Bear Cub looked big and very tough.

"Sure," said Rowdy. "Let's play tag."

"Okay," said Bear Cub. She winked at Young Wild Cat. "I'm it, and I'll catch you, Rowdy."

Bear Cub galloped toward Rowdy. Rowdy raced away as fast as he could. Pow! Bear Cub's paw caught Rowdy and knocked him ears over tail.

"Ow!" yelled Rowdy. "You play too rough. You hurt me."

"Tough beans!" Bear Cub yelled back. "You're it now, Rowdy."

Young Wild Cat yelled:
Rowdy can't catch me!
He can't even catch a flea!
Rowdy chased Young Wild Cat. Then he chased Bear Cub. He hopped and ran and hopped. But he couldn't catch either one.

At last, Rowdy stopped. Quick as a wink, Young Wild Cat sneaked up and spun Rowdy around like a top until he fell down dizzy.

"Tagged you again," shouted Young Wild Cat. "Now you're it twice over!"

Rowdy got back on his feet. He rubbed his ears. Then he rubbed his eyes.

"You guys are too rough for me," he said. "I'm going home."

"Too rough?" laughed Bear Cub. "Too rough for Rough Tough Rowdy?"

Young Wild Cat said, "Aw, we were just playing. Can't you take a joke, Rowdy? Or are you just a scaredy little bunny?"

Rowdy didn't answer.

Slowly, slowly, Rowdy hopped back home.
Very quietly he ate his lunch.

"Are you sick?" asked Mama Rabbit.

"Are you mad?" asked Rooter.

"Are you sad?" asked Rhoda.

"Did you lose your voice?" asked Margaret Rose.

But Rowdy didn't answer. His long ears drooped. His nose quivered.

After lunch, Mama Rabbit asked, "Want to tell me about it, son?"

Tears fell from Rowdy's big round eyes.

"I don't like it when friends play too rough," he sobbed. "It isn't any fun."

Mama Rabbit took Rowdy on her lap.

"How about when you are rough with your sisters and brothers?" she asked gently.

"I don't mean to be rough," whispered Rowdy. "I don't want to hurt anyone. But my paws want to push. And my feet want to kick and thump. I'm full of pushes and pounces and thumps!"

"I know," said Mama Rabbit softly. "But you've got to be boss of all those punches and pushes and pounces. You're the BIG BOSS!"

"Okay," sniffed Rowdy.

He cuddled closer to his mother's warm fur.

And for all the rest of that day, Rough Tough Rowdy didn't hurt anyone at all.

The next day, Rowdy made up a poem:

I'LL TRY TO BE GENTLER WHEN I PLAY

WITH THE OTHER BUNNIES EVERY DAY.

BUT WHEN I'M ALONE WITH ONLY ME,

I'LL BE POUNCY AND BOUNCY, WILD AND FREE,

AS THUMPY AND BUMPY AS I CAN BE!